WITHDRAWN from The Free Library of Philadelphia
Book contains theft-detection device that may set off alarm.

W9-AZO-970

The Cats Kids

The Cats Kids

written and illustrated by

Kay Chorao

Holiday House
New York

Copyright © 1998 by Kay Sproat Chorao
All rights reserved
Printed in the United States of America

FIRST EDITION

Library of Congress Cataloging-in-Publication Data
Chorao, Kay.
The Cats kids / written and illustrated by Kay Chorao.—1st ed.
p.   cm.
Summary: Jake Cats saves his runaway little brother, goes fishing for the family,
and helps his big sister prepare for the school play.
ISBN 0-8234-1405-1
[1. Cats—Fiction. 2. Brothers and sisters—Fiction.] I. Title.
PZ7.C4463Car   1998   98-3449   CIP   AC
[E]—dc21

Contents

LAWNCREST BRANCH

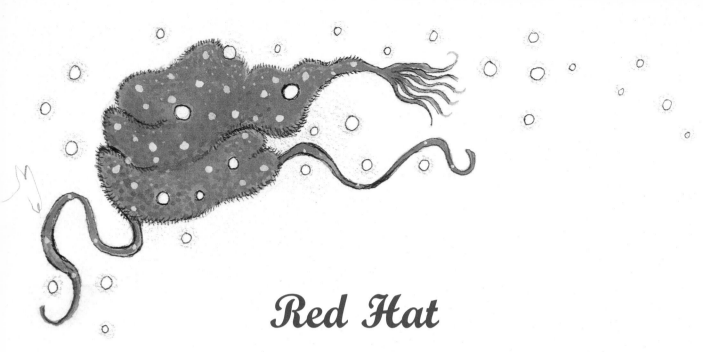

Red Hat

The Cats kids were all indoors.

Outside, snow fell like feathers from a giant pillow.

Trees and cars wore thick snow blankets.

"Let's go sledding," said Jake.

"I could fall off," said Sam, "or smash into a tree."

"You can sit on my lap. I will steer," said Jake.

"The snow is very deep. I could get lost," said Sam.

"I will give you my tall red hat," said Jake. "It will show above the snow."

"My paws will get cold," said Sam.

"You can wear my old rubber boots and my fuzzy mittens," said Jake.

Outside Sam tried to follow in Jake's paw prints.

He tripped.

"Pull me on the sled," begged Sam.

"You are such a baby," said Jake. But he pulled his
little brother on the sled.

When they reached the hill, Sam rolled off. "Too steep," he said.

Jake threw himself on the sled. "Hop on top," he said.

"You promised to *hold* me," whined Sam.

"You are such a baby," said Jake. But he held his little brother.

They whizzed down the hill.

Sam closed his eyes. He felt the ground fly by under the sled. He felt the snow zoom by his nose. He felt Jake's strong arms hold him tight.

"More," said Sam. "More."

They went down the hill again and again. And again.

Jake is a good brother, thought Sam. *He helps me dress. He gives me rides. He holds me tight when I am afraid.*

"I will walk home. You don't have to pull me," said Sam.

Jake smiled. He held Sam's paw.

Sam remembered hearing Jake ask Mama for money to buy a book.

"No," Mama had said. Then Jake had looked sad.

When they got home, Sam ran to his room. He grabbed his piggy bank.

"Where is Jake?" he asked his big sister, Martha.

"He went to buy a book," she said.

"But he needs my money," said Sam.

"No, Sammy, Mama paid him for baby-sitting you," said Martha.

"But Jake wasn't baby-sitting. He was playing with me," said Sam. "Jake likes me."

"No one wants to play with you. You are just a baby," said Martha. "Mama had to pay Jake."

Sam wanted to say *you are wrong*. But he remembered what Jake had said. "You are such a baby," he had said. "You are such a baby."

11

Tears rolled down Sam's furry face.

He ran to the door.

"I am not a baby. I am running away," he cried.

Martha giggled.

"Jake *does* like me," said Sam. "He does like me. And I am *not* a baby."

Snow blinded Sam's eyes. Wind froze his whiskers. Jake's old boots felt heavy. Sam's paws felt frozen. But he trudged on.

A fat lady bumped into Sam. "Watch where you are going," she yelled.

An old man poked Sam with his cane. "Move on, move on," he roared.

"Go home to your Mama," said a lady pushing a stroller.

Then Sam reached a busy street.

"Red is stop. Green is go," Sam whispered to himself.

The light turned green.

Sam had never crossed a street alone.

He felt his heart pound.

He put one foot on the street.

He heard Mama's voice in his head. "Never, never cross the street alone," it said.

A motorcycle shot by.

Sam jumped out of the way, falling into a snow pile.

He tried to pull himself out, but a snowplow came by. It threw more snow on Sam. He was almost buried. Sam tried to climb out, but the snow was too deep.

Sam began to cry. Then he began to howl. He howled and howled.

"Where is that howling coming from?" asked a man with earmuffs.

"With this wind there is no telling," said another man.

"Poor soul," said a very old woman.

Sam howled and howled. He felt so tired. He felt so sad.
He felt so frozen. He stopped howling and cried silently.

"Ah, there you are," said a voice.

Sam knew that voice.

Arms reached through the snow.

Arms hugged Sam close.

Sam knew those arms. They made him feel safe.

"I would know your howling anywhere," said Jake.

"Then I saw your red hat!"

When Sam and Jake got home, Martha was crying. Mama had
punished her for letting Sam run away.

"I was so worried," said Mama. "I have been calling everyone.
I have been looking everywhere for you, Sammy."

She picked him up and wrapped him in a warm Mama-hug.

"But the rest of the day you must stay in your room all by yourself
and think about what you did," she said.

Sam went to his room.

Jake slipped in. "I bought two books, one for me and this one
for you, Sammy."

They made a tent out of Sam's quilt and curled inside. Jake read
the new book in a very quiet voice. Only Sammy heard.

Black Witch Hat

Jake put his head in the refrigerator.

"I'm hungry," he said. "Where is my fish?"

"Papa ate it," said Mama.

"But I caught it. It was mine," said Jake.

"Never mind. Have this nice egg salad sandwich," said Mama.

Jake took the sandwich and ran outdoors. He climbed to the top of the maple tree. A spring breeze whispered through the leaves. Jake swayed back and forth on a branch, frowning at his sandwich.

Martha came out of the house. "Mama wants you to help Papa mow the front lawn."

"Papa ate my fish," said Jake, taking a teeny-tiny bite of his egg salad.

"Mama says right now," said Martha. "She means right this minute." Martha stamped her foot.

"You are not my boss," said Jake.

"You are such a baby," said Martha.

The screen door slammed. Sam ran out. "Mama says Papa is melting. She wants Jake to help Papa."

"Why do *I* have to help?" asked Jake.

"You are the big boy," said Sam.

"Martha says I am a baby. So *you* go, Martha," said Jake.

"I'm telling Mama," said Martha, running back to the house.

"If Papa melts he will be all gone," said Sam.

"Papa is not a popsicle," said Jake.

The screen door slammed again. Martha ran to the swing.

"Now you have done it," she said.

"Papa melted," howled Sam.

"Yes," said Martha. "Papa melted. It is all Jake's fault."

Sam began to cry. "Mama," he cried, running to the house.

"Now, Jake, see what you have done?" said Martha.

Jake ran around the house to help Papa. There, at the edge
of the lawn was the mower. But no Papa.

"Uh-oh," thought Jake. Maybe Papa *had* melted. He ran into
the woods, through the shadows that flickered black and scary.

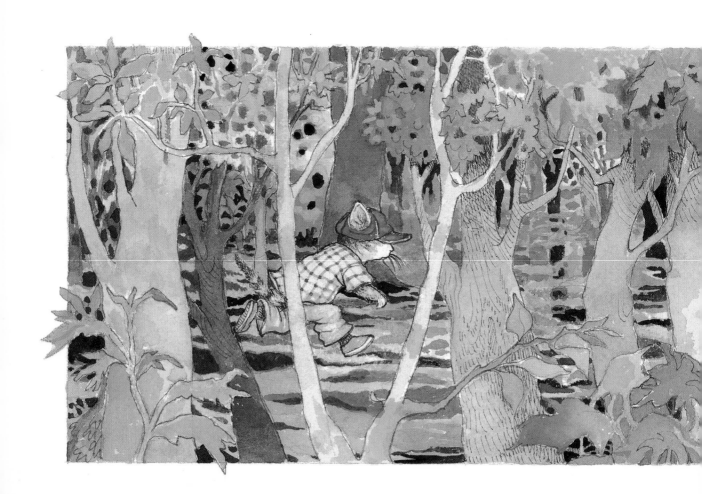

Jake ran until he reached the shed by the river. When Papa
was there the river was bright and friendly. Today it rumbled
past rocks like shiny teeth. When Papa was there the shed was cozy.
Today it was shadowy dark. And the door was open!

Uh-oh, someone broke in, thought Jake.

He tip-toed through the door.

The shed was empty.

Jake grabbed a fishing pole and ran out. He ran to the rowboat under the willow tree. He climbed in and rowed away.

I will catch lots of fish for Mama and Papa and Martha and Sam so they won't be mad at me anymore, thought Jake.

Jake knew where the fish hid. Papa had taught him. He knew how to cast his line and reel it in. Jake rowed hard and the little boat rounded a curve.

There, standing in hip boots, was a giant woman wearing a big floppy witch hat.

The thief? thought Jake. *Or maybe a* river witch? He didn't wait to find out. He turned the boat and rowed back around the curve. He rowed and rowed until he found a wide, deep, secret place.

First Jake caught a little fish, just right for Sam. Then he caught a big one, just right for Papa. The sun was falling low in the sky when Jake caught a middle-sized fish, just right for Mama.

Now he had a present for everyone but Martha.

The sun was sinking lower and lower. The sky was streaked with raspberry red. Soon it would be dark. He could get lost and the river witch might find him.

Just as Jake was ready to leave, a big fish tugged at his line. Quickly he reeled it in. Then he rowed as fast as he could to the old willow tree. Beside the tree lay Papa's fishing cap. Jake stuffed the fish into Papa's cap and ran to the shed. The door was shut. Maybe the river witch was inside!

Jake ran. He ran and stumbled and ran some more. Twigs snapped against his face. Fallen branches tripped his feet. But he hugged the fish in Papa's hat and kept running through the dark woods.

At last he stumbled into his own backyard. There, leaning over Papa's vegetable garden, was THE RIVER WITCH!

Jake froze, too scared to run.

She stood up and turned around.

It was *Papa!* Papa was wearing a big witch hat.

"Hi, Jake. Don't you know me in Mama's beach hat?"

Jake began to laugh.

Papa laughed, too. "I got so warm mowing that Mama made me wear her new sun hat. I couldn't find my own cap."

"I found it," Jake said, holding up the cap.

"And it's full of fish," said Papa. "We both played hookey, didn't we?"

"I'm sorry I didn't help you mow," said Jake.

"I'm sorry I ate your fish," said Papa. "But now we have plenty for everyone."

Then Papa took Jake's paw in his big one and together
they walked into the house. Mama cooked a delicious fish dinner.
Jake ate three fish.

The next morning, before anyone else was awake,
Jake mowed the lawn.

Orange Dress

Outside the Cats' house leaves drifted from the trees.

"I want my dress to be as orange as those leaves," said Martha.

Jake looked up from his writing pad.

"What dress?" he asked.

"The dress I will wear in the school play," said Martha.

"The school play. The school play. I'm sick of hearing about the school play," Jake said.

"Little brothers," sniffed Martha.

Sam came in. "I want to play, too," he said.

"Not play like hide-and-seek," said Martha. "Play like acting. Like on TV. Like in movies."

Sam blinked. "I play with Binky," he said, holding up his doll.

Martha rolled her eyes. "Little brothers," she said again.

The next day Martha went to the store with Mama.
They bought two yards of orange cotton.

When they got home Martha drew a picture. "Like this, Mama.
It must be very beautiful, because I am going to be a famous actress."

Mama drew on the cotton with white chalk, and Martha helped her
cut along the lines. They pinned the pieces in place. Then Mama
showed Martha how to work the sewing machine and they stitched
the pieces together.

"My orange dress," purred Martha. She tried it on.
"Ummmmm," said Mama. "Maybe with a little ruffle."
Martha found some old lace curtains in the rag bag.
Mama made them into ruffles.
"Wheee," yelled Martha. "Now I look like a real princess."

Martha tried to practice her lines.

"It's hard all alone. Will you help, Jake?"

"I'm busy writing," said Jake.

"Please?"

"Oh, all right," grumbled Jake.

Martha read her lines.

She swept across the floor, dipping and twirling.

"Don't yell," said Jake, "and stop jumping around."

"What do you know?" asked Martha.

"Cleomia is a wood elf," said Jake, "not a jack-in-the-box."

"Cleomia is a princess," said Martha. "Anyway, I have an orange princess dress, so that's that."

All week Martha practiced her lines with Jake.

On Friday she stuffed the orange dress into her backpack.

"Why are you doing that?" asked Mama.

"Today is tryout day for the school play," said Martha.

"Tryouts? I thought you *had* the part," said Mama.

"Oh, no," groaned Jake. "All that time wasted." He frowned at Martha.

"I will get the part. You will see. At three o'clock on the school stage."

She twirled out the door. "Say good-bye, Cleomia," she called.

"Good-bye, Cleomia," said Mama.

"Good-bye, clean-me-off," said Sam.

Martha did her princess walk all the way to school.

At three o'clock Martha was the first in line.

Jake peeked in. He watched children arrive. He watched Martha pull her orange dress over her blue jeans.

She looked like a pumpkin.

Mrs. Spoon stood on the stage. She called a few children to say their lines. Minnie was good. So were Ginger and Rose. Then it was Martha's turn.

She twirled to show off her orange dress.

A few children giggled.

Martha danced into center stage. Suddenly she looked scared. She was all alone. Everyone was staring at her.

Jake crept closer.

He saw the ruffles on her dress shake and shiver. He saw her face, terrified. Martha had never stood all alone on a stage with everyone looking at her.

Jake crept closer.

Martha looked at Jake for help. He crept almost to her side. He remembered all her lines. First he said them, then she repeated them.

His voice gave Martha courage. Soon she was saying her lines in her loud actress voice. All the while she dipped and twirled.

When she and Jake finished, Mrs. Spoon clapped her paws.

Martha did a curtsey.

Someone giggled.

"I do believe we have our Cleomia," beamed Mrs. Spoon.

Minnie, Ginger, and Rose ran back on stage.

"All these girls were wonderful, weren't they?" asked Mrs. Spoon.

There was a little applause.

"But today we found a hidden talent," she said.

Then she plucked Jake from the shadows.

"Our winner," she announced.

Everyone clapped.

Everyone but Martha.

She ran. She ran all the way home in her orange dress.

No one could comfort her.

Mama tried, but Martha wiggled out of her arms.

Papa tried, but Martha ran to her room.

"You can play with Binky," said Sam. But Martha took Binky and threw him across her room. Sam ran away, howling.

When Jake came home, Martha stomped to his room.

"I never want to see you again," she cried. "You stole my part."

Martha looked very angry.

Jake hid his head under a pillow.

Martha snatched the pillow.

Jake looked up. He was crying.

"She thought I was a *girl*," he said.

Martha stopped looking so angry.

"I can't ever go to school again," cried Jake. "I can't ever go *outside* again."

Martha sat next to Jake. "Of course you can. You are the smartest little brother ever."

"But everyone laughed at me. She thought I was a girl," said Jake.

"Someday no one will laugh, when you are a famous writer," said Martha. "Besides, they laughed at me, too."

"I know," said Jake.

Then they sat side by side, not saying a word for a very long time.

"Can I play, too?" asked Sam, wandering in.

"We can all play together," said Jake. "I will write a play just for us."

"We can put it on in our backyard," said Martha.

"It will be all about a pumpkin who turns into a princess," said Jake.

"That will be ME," said Martha, hopping off the bed and doing a fancy spin.

So one bright Saturday they gave a play in
their backyard on a carpet of autumn leaves.
Jake was the prince and Martha was the
beautiful princess.

Everyone clapped and clapped.

Sam got to be the frog.

They clapped for him, too.

THE
END

LAWNCREST BRANCH

THE FREE LIBRARY OF PHILADELPHIA

3 2222 10967 3220

X

MAY   2000

28 12-03
18 12/01.